This book belongs to

_____

Disney

Dumbo

★

The Story of Dumbo

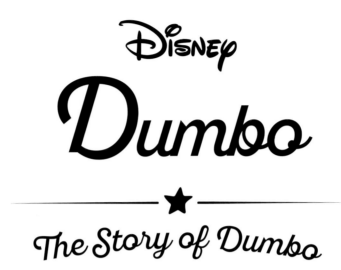

Disney

Dumbo

★

The Story of Dumbo

Bath · New York · Cologne · Melbourne · Delhi
Hong Kong · Shenzhen · Singapore

This edition published by Parragon Books Ltd in 2016
and distributed by

Parragon Inc.
440 Park Avenue South, 13th Floor
New York, NY 10016
www.parragon.com

ISBN 978-1-4748-5040-7

Printed in China

Don't just fly, soar!

As the evening stars shone brightly, a flock of storks flew across the sky. In their beaks they carried special bundles over a big circus. At just the right moment, the storks released their very important deliveries.
The bundles gently floated down to the circus tents.

One by one, the bundles opened, revealing newborn animals. Mrs. Jumbo, the elephant, waited anxiously for hers. She saw a kangaroo, a hippopotamus, a giraffe, a tiger, and two baby bears, who were all greeted with love by their mothers. Even after the last bundle fell, Mrs. Jumbo hopefully watched the sky.

The next morning, the animals boarded the circus train.
The circus would stop at many towns.
Casey Junior, the train engine, blew his whistle proudly
as the train pulled away.

Way up high, a very tired stork was sitting on a cloud.
His heavy bundle was right next to him. Mr. Stork was lost and
very late. He needed to find Mrs. Jumbo. Suddenly, he heard the
happy whistle of Casey Junior. "That's it!" shouted Mr. Stork.
Delighted, he grabbed the bundle and flew quickly toward the
circus train.

The stork landed on the train and walked along the roof. He called out for Mrs. Jumbo. The lady elephants began waving their trunks at him. "Yoo-hoo!" they shouted.

Mr. Stork delicately set down the bundle in front of Mrs. Jumbo. She was overjoyed. Her baby had finally arrived! After completing his delivery paperwork, the stork asked if she had a name picked out. "Jumbo Junior," Mrs. Jumbo declared.

Mrs. Jumbo eagerly untied the bundle. There he was! Her Jumbo Junior. He was more adorable then she could have imagined. She immediately fell in love.

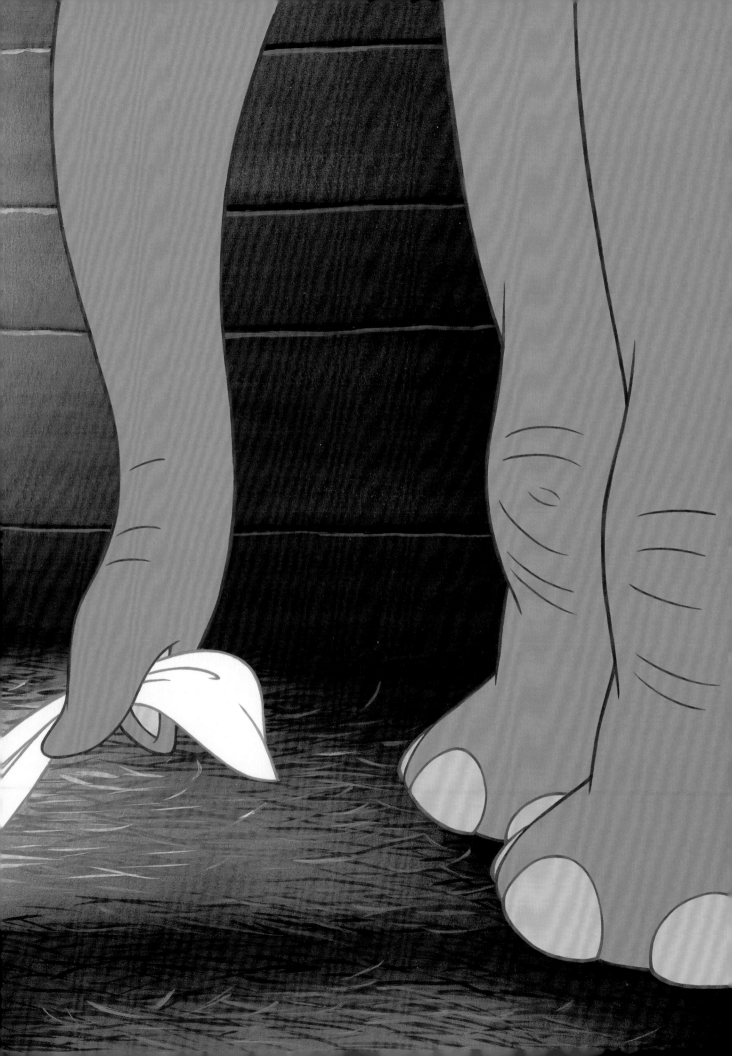

Suddenly, the baby elephant sneezed, causing his ears to unfold completely. They were enormous!

The lady elephants began making mean jokes about him. Laughing, they gave the little one a nickname: Dumbo.

Angry at the teasing from the other elephants,
Mrs. Jumbo whisked her baby away. She cradled
him. She loved everything about him, especially his
big ears. Dumbo smiled. He felt safe, warm, and
happy with his mother.

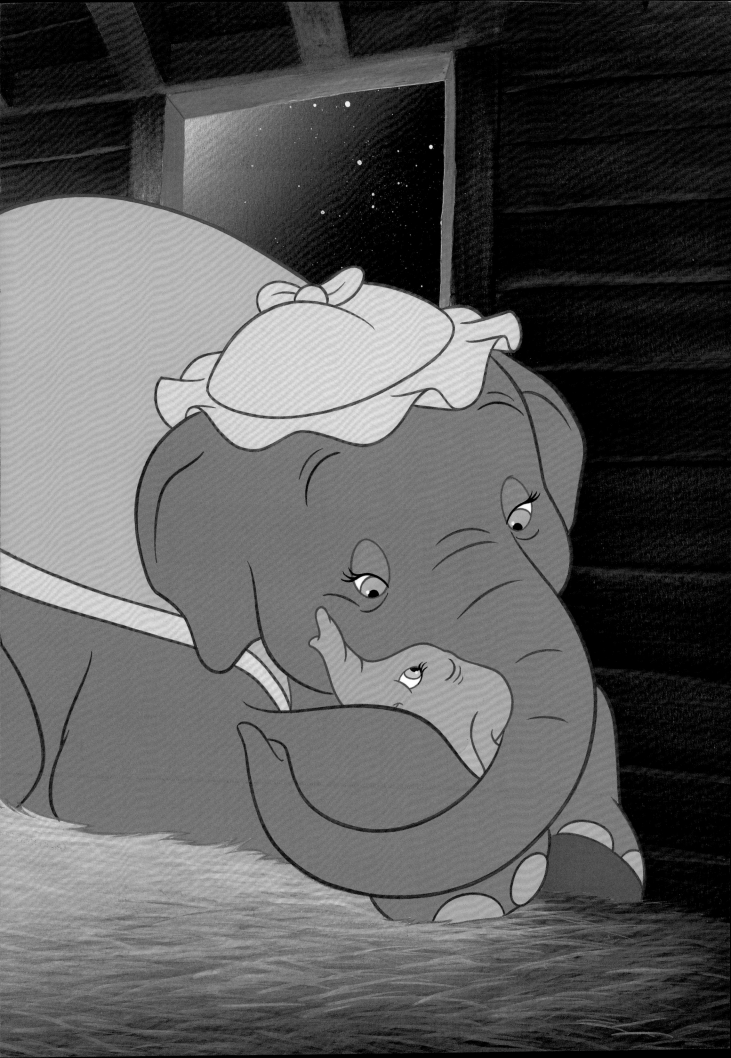

The next day, the train came to a stop and the elephants set up the Big Top tent. The townspeople lined the street to watch the Ringmaster lead a parade. The crowd cheered the animal wagons, which housed a lion, tigers, and a gorilla that thumped its mighty chest. There were clowns, too, whose silly antics made everyone laugh.

A proud Mrs. Jumbo marched down the street. Dumbo held on to his mother's tail, his face beaming with excitement. The townspeople thought he was adorable. But when Dumbo tripped over his big, floppy ears and fell into a puddle of mud, everyone laughed.

Back at the tent, Mrs. Jumbo gave Dumbo a bubble bath and got him squeaky clean. A group of young boys entered the tent and began making fun of Dumbo. One of the mean boys grabbed Dumbo's ear and began blowing into it. Dumbo tried to hide behind his mother's leg.

Dumbo's mother trumpeted with anger. She wanted to defend herself and her son from the mean boys. Mrs. Jumbo grabbed a bale of hay, and the boys began to scream and run.

The Ringmaster ordered his men to capture Mrs. Jumbo.
They threw ropes around her so that she couldn't move.
Then the Ringmaster took little Dumbo from his mother,
who bellowed with anger and fright.

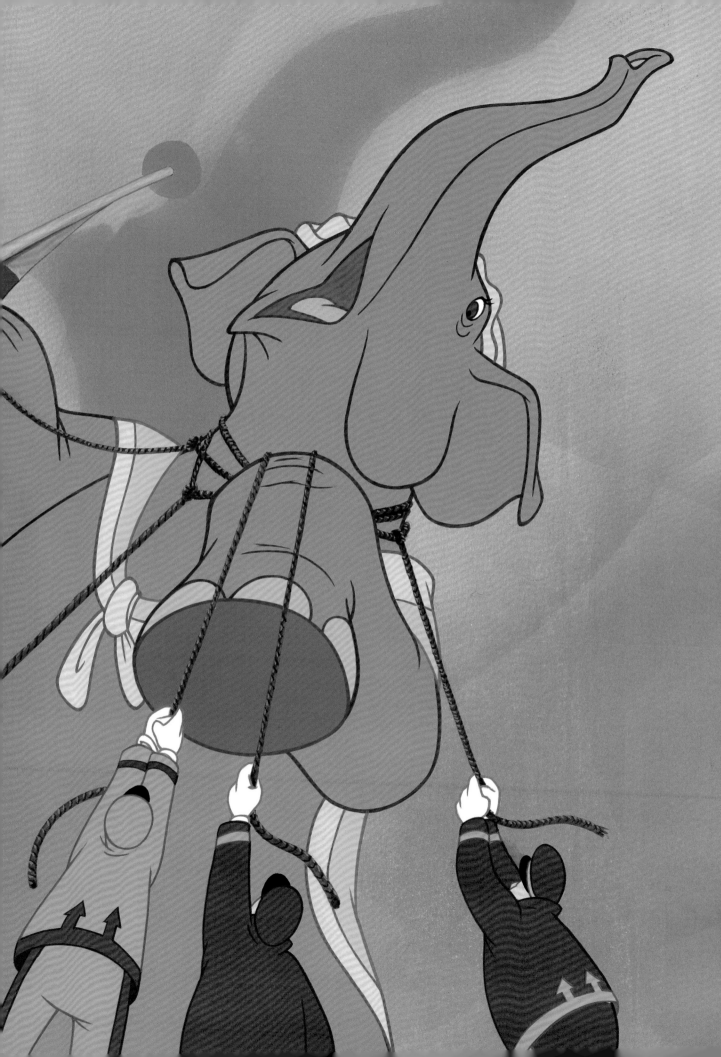

Dumbo's mother was worried about her little one. All she wanted was to be close to him again.

Dumbo didn't understand why they had taken his mother. He tried to join the other elephants, but they turned their backs on him. Then they starting talking about Mrs. Jumbo and the trouble she was in. They blamed everything on Dumbo and his big ears.

Timothy Q. Mouse, a smart little fellow who traveled with the circus, felt sorry for Dumbo. "Poor little guy," he said to himself. "Not a friend in the world." Timothy decided it was up to him to help Dumbo.

When the elephants saw Timothy, they shrieked in terror. There was, after all, only one thing in the world that could really scare an elephant: a mouse. Timothy wiggled his nose and made funny faces at them. As they reacted with alarm, Timothy laughed and ran to find Dumbo.

Dumbo was hiding in a bale of hay. He didn't want to talk to Timothy at first. But Timothy fed Dumbo a delicious peanut and said, "I think your ears are beautiful." Dumbo smiled. He had made his first friend.

Timothy told Dumbo that he would help Dumbo become a circus star. "Dumbo the Great!" he shouted. Later, Timothy heard the Ringmaster wondering what would happen if all the circus elephants climbed on top of each other to form a pyramid.

When the Ringmaster went to sleep, Timothy snuck into his tent. Hiding beneath a sheet like a ghost, the mouse whispered into the Ringmaster's ear. He suggested that the big circus act should end with the baby elephant jumping on top of the giant elephant pyramid. "Dumbo!" Timothy whispered. "Dumbo!"

The next night, the Ringmaster announced that the elephants were about to do something amazing. Seven enormous elephants would balance on top of a small, round ball. It would be stupendous!

Dumbo's job was to run into the
ring, jump on a springboard, and
land on top of the elephant pyramid.
But when Dumbo practiced his run,
he tripped over his big ears. Thinking
fast, Timothy tied Dumbo's ears up
over his head. It was showtime!

"Ladies and gentlemen!" the Ringmaster shouted.
"I give you . . . Dumbo!" The little elephant dashed into the
ring. But just as he was about to jump onto the board that
would launch him high into the air, Dumbo's ears came loose.
He tripped over them and flew forward . . .

. . . smashing against the red ball on which the elephants were balanced.

As the ball began to roll, the elephants began to wobble. They swayed left and then right. Trumpeting with fear, they hung on bravely.

Finally, the pyramid of elephants tumbled down. They flew across the Big Top, hitting the wires and poles that held the tent up. There was a loud crack as the wooden pole in the center of the tent snapped in two. The Big Top began to fall.

The audience fled to safety as the giant tent floated to the ground. This was an evening at the circus that no one would ever forget!

After everyone boarded, the circus train
chugged into the night.

Inside, the elephants were wrapped in
bandages. They blamed Dumbo for all
that had happened. He was no longer
welcome in the elephant train car.

So Dumbo started working with the circus clowns. For their big show, he was dressed up like a baby and placed at the top of a burning building. The clowns were dressed as very silly firemen!

At the end of the act, Dumbo jumped from the burning building. He landed in a giant bucket filled with thick white plaster. Everyone laughed as the little elephant rose up out of the tub, his face covered in goop.

Timothy did his best to cheer up Dumbo. He gave him a bath and told him how well he had done. Dumbo wouldn't listen. He missed his mother. Luckily, Timothy had a special surprise in mind for his good friend Dumbo.

Timothy took Dumbo to see his mother! Mrs. Jumbo
was still locked up, but she was able to put her trunk
through the wagon window and cradle her baby.
Dumbo smiled as she gently rocked him.

Dumbo cried a little after seeing his mother.
All he wanted was to be with her. Once he lay down
to sleep, he began to have the strangest dream.
In the dream, he was blowing bubbles. Soon, the
bubbles looked just like elephants—elephants that
danced and flew!

The next morning, Timothy tried to convince Dumbo that he could fly just like a bird. He said Dumbo's ears were so big, they were like wings. Dumbo wasn't so sure, but he trusted Timothy. He would try to fly.

In the next show, Dumbo performed once again with the clowns. They wanted him to leap from the burning building. But this time, Timothy had given a feather to Dumbo. Timothy said it was a magic feather that would help him fly. Holding it tightly, Dumbo got ready to jump.

It worked! Dumbo and Timothy soared through the
air. But halfway to the bottom, Dumbo lost his grip on
the magic feather. Without it, he couldn't fly. He and
Timothy were falling!

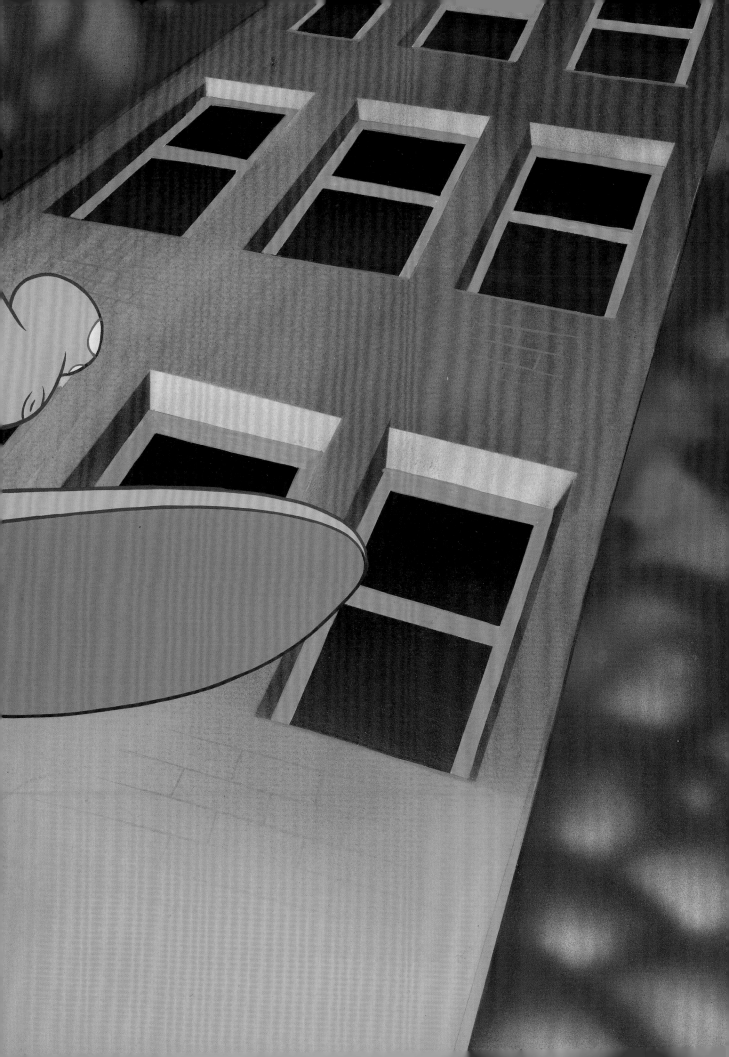

With the wind whistling past as they sped toward the ground, Timothy quickly told Dumbo that the magic feather wasn't real. He didn't need it. All he had to do was believe in himself.

Whoosh! Dumbo opened his ears just before he hit the ground. The clowns, the Ringmaster, and the audience watched him in amazement. Timothy shouted for joy as Dumbo flew up, down, and all around the Big Top. He was a flying elephant!

Then Dumbo began to play. He chased the clowns until they all jumped into a barrel of water. He scooped up a bunch of peanuts and hurled them at the elephants. "You're making history!" Timothy declared.

In the days that followed, Dumbo became the most famous elephant in the world. The circus was more popular than ever. People came from all over to see the little elephant fly. Timothy, who was now Dumbo's manager, became famous, too.

The two best friends made
history around the world!

The Ringmaster freed Dumbo's mother and gave her a fancy car at the end of the circus train to share with her son. For Dumbo, there was nothing more wonderful than being with his mother. again.

When she hugged him tight, he was the happiest elephant in the world. Even though Dumbo was now a star, he would always be Mrs. Jumbo's baby.

The End